Jacob Greenberg

THE LITTLE GIANT

WRITTEN AND ILLUSTRATED BY

SERGIO RUZZIER

LAURA GERINGER BOOKS

An Imprint of HarperCollinsPublishers

The Little Giant
Copyright © 2004 by Sergio Ruzzier
Manufactured in China. All rights reserved.
www.harperchildrens.com

Library of Congress Cataloging-in-Publication Data
Ruzzier, Sergio.
The little giant / written and illustrated by Sergio Ruzzier.
p.   cm.
Summary: When a little giant meets a big dwarf, they realize
they are more alike than they seem.
ISBN 0-06-052951-2 —ISBN 0-06-052952-0 (lib. bdg.)
[1. Size—Fiction.   2. Friendship—Fiction.   3. Giants—
Fiction.   4. Dwarfs—Fiction.] I. Title.
PZ7.R9475 Li 2004   [E]—dc21   2002012948   CIP   AC
Typography by Alicia Mikles
1 2 3 4 5 6 7 8 9 10

First Edition

For Viola

Deep in the Tappari Mountains there lived a village of giants.

As one would expect from giants, they were very tall and very big in every way. Their legs and arms were long, their chests were vast, and their heads were enormous.

But one of them was not very tall
or very big at all.

Angelino de' Grandi
was a little giant.

Because of his size, Angelino was ignored
by the other giants. He felt sad and lonely.

One day Angelino decided to leave. He filled his favorite glass with fresh water, in case he got thirsty, and left the Tappari Mountains for the first time in his life.

After a long walk he had finished his water,
but he was still thirsty—and very tired.

Soon he came to a beautiful pond,
with water as clear as crystal.

Bending over to fill his glass, Angelino took a moment to observe his reflection in the pond. "Something is not right," he thought.

The reflection emerged from the water. It looked exactly like Angelino.

"Are you a little giant?" Angelino asked.

"No," the reflection answered. "My name is Osvaldo Curti, and I am a big dwarf.

"I have left my village because the other dwarfs don't like me. They think I am too tall."
"I have left my village also! The other giants think I am too small!" Angelino cried.

The two hugged. They were happy
to have found one another.

And so Angelino and Osvaldo decided
to live together, by the clear pond.

They talked of serious matters and silly things, took long walks, read books, and played in the pond, gently floating side by side, staring at the immense sky above them. The two friends couldn't ask for a better life.

But one day they received some bad news.

A war had broken out between the dwarfs and the giants. The giants were strong and mighty, but the dwarfs were many and well armed.

Angelino and Osvaldo left their peaceful
pond and headed for the battlefield.
They knew they had to do something to
stop the war, but they didn't know what.

Overwhelmed by the fury of the fight,
they soon lost one another.

Angelino found himself among the dwarfs,
where they mistook him for Osvaldo.

"Osvaldo!" they shouted. "Have you come to help us fight the giants?"
"I am Angelino," he said, "and I myself am a giant!"

In the meantime Osvaldo found himself among
the giants, who mistook him for Angelino.

"Angelino!" they shouted. "Have you come to help us fight the dwarfs?"
"I am Osvaldo," he said, "and I myself am a dwarf!"

The dwarfs and the giants were shocked.
Angelino and Osvaldo were identical, and
yet one was a giant and one was a dwarf!

How could the giants and the dwarfs keep fighting, when no one could tell one from the other?

So the giants and the dwarfs went back to their own villages, each wishing the others all the best.

Angelino and Osvaldo returned to their beautiful pond and lived happily together, reading books, taking long walks, and playing in the pond, gently floating side by side, talking of silly matters and serious things.

Years later they forgot which one was the little giant and which was the big dwarf.